The Miraculous Escape

Evincepub Publishing

Parijat Extension, Bilaspur, Chhattisgarh 495001
First Published by Evincepub Publishing 2022

ISBN: 978-93-5446-802-5

The Miraculous Escape

Wrapped up with poetry on destiny, faith, hope and courage.

Adv. Shivangini Jindal

DEDICATION

To my parents, Mr. Pradeep Jindal & Mrs. Rajmani Jindal.

My Father

A man with immense magnanimity and wit,
Never giving up on his stern morals and grit,
A man whose work is his passion,
Irrespective of the occasion,
A businessman who doesn't teach but leads by being an example,
For he knows how to keep up his organization's handle,
No matter what obstructions and tests the fate has thrown,
He has never feared the unknown and always outgrown,
A man who has been an exceptionally great son,
With sincerity and honesty he ensured their comfort is done,
Regardless of how hard the run,
A man who has been a religious giver to the poor and needy,
As opposed to the nasty and greedy,
Known for his humility and down to earth nature,
It ought to be his compass to navigate through the vicissitudes
thrown by the Maker,
Earnestly praying for your choicest benedictions,
For I am your reflection,
And you my protection,
Proudly I call you my Father,
Whose life is worth a million dollar.

My Mother

A woman of strict principles and honesty,
Being no less than an avatar of the Almighty,
A woman always ready to help others,
She's no less than a queen for her brothers,
Being the youngest amongst all her siblings,
She led the way by her own winnings,
A woman who was a great daughter,
For she never failed to make her family applaud her,
An advocate and a distinguished tax consultant,
She's always been triumphant,
Notwithstanding what challenges life has thrown,
She's never frown,
For her faith in the Lord has always grown,
Wholeheartedly praying for her spouse and her daughter,
She keeps up their laughter,
Not that I share all my emotions with her,
Or she discloses all her woes to me,
Yet we both end up reading the sensations of each other's heart,
Even if we're miles apart,
For I am an inseparable part of her body and soul which can never depart,

Proudly I call her my Mother,
Like her there is no other.

PREFACE

There are certain chapters in life which no matter how hard you try, can't be skipped. You have to read row after row, encounter every person you are destined to meet and undergo whatever trials the fate has kept on the horizon for you. Definitely, all of them are not going to be joyous; some will make you sob and scream from days to weeks while others may make you smile the widest for months ahead. For you have to keep walking ahead because, 'Life is nothing but the name of efforts to get the answers'.

Undoubtedly even the biggest of the disasters do get resolved with passing time, even though you are suffering or in despair. For you must always remember being compassionate towards your own self, that's the only possible way to push ahead and allow the cosmos to move things at its own pace. You do not always have to yearn and struggle to find an explanation for the circumstances you are actually in. As more often than not it is immensely prudent to accept that there isn't just one and maybe saying, 'God knows why' is all the slogan you need to tell yourself to walk ahead.

In life, there are possibly two sounds that are scrambling for your observation. Predominantly, the 'sound of faith and conviction' and secondarily is the 'sound of failure and downfall.' If you listen attentively, you'll discover the former saying, 'The Almighty has a plan, he will make a way and he will undoubtedly heal'. Whereas the latter would say, 'I am not well equipped, I cannot do anything and all I have lined ahead are worse days'.

I firmly believe that while staggering under heavy pressure the only output port to it is resisting with immense patience; as doing the contrary is less likely to serve you well.

Every dip of your life is planned by the Lord to teach you how to breathe submerged. Allow it to inculcate that in you until it departs and it actually won't depart until it fulfills its job.

People around you shall be all warmed up to tuition you with maxims like, 'what has to happen will happen', 'this is your destiny' and so on and so forth. Get up and fight because that is what is required to be done. For sometimes you do not have a choice. Persist by taking those baby steps towards the desired goal and watch yourself shining like the sun firing up the sky with dazzling colors. Irrefutably, life is an everlasting string of relay struggles. Tutor yourself in every rough phase so that you become stronger or rather more eligible to face the next one.

Passthroughs can be defined by periods, dates, spells or even by destinations; as most often they are. But I feel it's complex and stern for me to tell you the story of my life on those footings, for its nothing but this conception of time that has always dodged me.

'The Miraculous Escape' is about my journey of rescuing my parents during the second wave of the pandemic; COVID-19 (April 2021 - July 2021). It's about moments of the day I saw my parents esp. my Father fighting for his every breath, times when I saw him lying in a prone position for days and days without uttering a single word only to maintain the saturation balance to finally seeing him overcome the fear of losing his breath upon removing the oxygen mask. With his indomitable grit he reiterated that irrespective of the disaster, a strong will power can make even the hardest mountains bend.

It also reveals about my peaks and troughs, elevations and depressions all throughout the journey when I myself was COVID-19 positive. The entire journey along with the rollercoaster of emotions I dealt with; have been described in a poetic format in over 100 poems depending on each phase and how the choicest benedictions of the Almighty helped me rescue them.

ACKNOWLEDGEMENTS

First of all, I would like to express my gratitude to Lord Shiva (Mahadev) for enabling me to not only write but also complete this book.

Successful completion of any book isn't the work of any one but many. Ergo, who have been directly or indirectly been a reason of my strength during the harsh phase in addition to the motivation to write this book.

Heartfelt gratitude to my parents for being the inspiration behind this book.

I want to thank my Guru ji for his blessings, strength and guidance which illuminated our path.

My late maternal and paternal grandparents for showering their blessings from above.

My words shall always be less to express the intensity and magnitude of my gratitude towards **"Dr. Janki Nandan Agarwal"** and his entire medical team.

It is worth stressing that his remarks on his initial visit were, 'He (my Father) will be on his feet in next 5 days', clearly outlined his enormous and gigantic confidence in his abilities to rescue his patients irrespective of the condition. From answering incessant patient calls requiring his help to handling them in case of their contingencies along with running from one junction to another notwithstanding the distance; he justified every word of his 'medical oath'. It was his aura, confidence and his presence that was no less than a source of protection for my parents. His medication eradicated the virus but his demeanor and conviction made us win the grueling, exhausting and painful battle. My words shall always be less to express my sense of obligation and indebtedness for he was no less than a ‘heavenly messenger’ sent specially by the Almighty to save innumerable families from a possible heartbreak.

From arranging IV equipment to medicines to their punctual delivery at our doorstep with just an easy call; needless to mention are his teams inexorable and unbending efforts to ensure our relief and well-being. To say the least, he reiterated that none is unattainable provided the diligences and attempts are strong and eternal.

Also I am grateful to Adv. Shri Varun Khanna, Adv. Nitika Khanna, Adv. Shri H.C.Bhatia, Late Adv. Shri Raj K Batra, Adv. Shri N. K.Gulati, Adv Shri Sanjay Sharma and the entire team of STBA for being a pillar of strength to my mother. It goes without saying that it wouldn't have been possible without the relentless efforts and unsurpassed grit of them.

From getting 'life saving' oxygen cylinders arranged to getting the rarest available flowmeter for oxygen cylinder; their support prayers, toils and sincere blessings turned the impossible into possible.

Finally, yet importantly I would like to evince my genuine and hearty gratitude towards all my relatives, near and dear ones and my close friends for being there to escort my ways whenever I felt lost. For they were the reason I could hold my horses and come up with this book.

ABOUT THE AUTHOR

Shivangini Jindal is an Advocate by profession. She completed her BA LLB (Hons) from Amity Law School, Delhi affiliated to Guru Gobind Singh Indraprastha University (GGSIPU) in 2018. She is also a rank holder in Diploma in Labour Laws and Labour Welfare (DLL & LW).

She has skilled herself in various branches viz Arbitration and Corporate by means of various trainings and externships with numerous Justices of High Court of Delhi and other elite legal firms.

Ahead of conceptualizing and envisioning the idea of sharing my voyage of relay struggles amid the COVID-19 second wave in a poetic format or before undergoing that tempestuous phase; I believe I was too callow and candid. Unenlightened and unknowing about multifarious expensive lessons of life. As goes the popular dictum that, 'Customarily life shoots such challenges and trials at us that no manual would assist'. This adage manifested itself verbatim. From my stand point this incident was nothing but a submerged dive plotted by the concerted action of the Almighty and the fate; to edify and enlighten me with those mantras and pearls of wisdom which conversely would have been too paradoxical to acquire. Nonetheless, I have also attempted to evince and highlight the same via a poem titled 'An Event That Changed Me' for the ease of all the readers.

I foresee this book to be an encouragement and source of vigor for any individual battling under or with whatever ravages of time to keep their chin up considering it to be a transitional phase which would in a short span depart. Meanwhile you must believe in yourself and in voluminousness and greatness of the plan of the Almighty. In the event of doubts, lean your head full of anxieties and questions in the house of God; for he is sure to signal you of a possible path.

CONTENTS

NATURE'S OCEAN CHURNING

The question - answer series started like this,
When my heart told me we have things untold,
We are together even though we are not,
With tears in my eyes, I said, 'Oh heart, what is it that made this nature cry to us'?
He whispered softly to my ear,
The series of your wishes went like this,
Having found them today, you drowned yourself,
For playing with the nature,
Humans cry all their lives.

Bearing the growing human race's,
Innumerable, unbearable and unspeakable misdeeds,
If not today, then tomorrow the nature had to be angry,
Seeing the future of the mankind in dark, if not today then tomorrow the nature had to remark,
In the greed of luxury the mankind made a big mistake,
In the desire to touch the sky,
He released the dust so high,
For playing with the nature,
Humans cry all their lives.

Meeting of the sky and the earth had to happen tomorrow if not today,
The tiny house of the birds had to be built once again if not today then tomorrow,
Like a Mother's love my Earth had to show me the right path,
If not today then tomorrow the basic mantra of living in harsh times it had to tell,
For playing with the nature,
Humans cry all their lives.

Holy Ganges flowing from the hair of Lord Mahadev, the God of gods was to be incarnated,
Like Mahishasur, Durgasur and Dhumravilochana, Goddess Durga had to destroy the evil deeds of human beings,
If not today then tomorrow the human race had to be reflected in the water of the churning of the ocean,
For playing with the nature,
Humans cry all their lives.

Music is in each particle of the nature today,
Let the cuckoo take a check today!
Why don't we smile with them today?
For everyday they rejoice our houses,
It is the flowers that make the valleys fragrant,
My Mother Earth fragrances every moment by filling them in its lap,

For playing with the nature,
Humans cry all their lives.

Supposedly something is different this time,
If you want, you can share it even today,
The only request is for silence,
Because human beings are injured by the arrow of ego- birth by birth,
Silence has a different role this time,
Because human's livelihood does not run without nature,
For playing with the nature,
Humans cry all their lives.
This is the call of the one who wore the cover of silence for many years,
This is the call of the one who wore the cover of silence for many years,
Get up! Our Mother Earth is calling,
For if you don't wake up now, then the entire human race will repent.

THE MIRACLE WORKER

The one having a heart of gold,
Their spirit is saintly and personality bold,
Their endeavor is their passion,
Which makes them save lives;
With immense compassion,
Persisting under heavy pressure in the best possible way,
They carry the weight of numerous blames and allegations without a word of say,
From morning to afternoon shifts; to innumerable sleepless nights,
They say a big "NO-NO" to all sorts of fights,
When in the pool of death you're drowning,
They are the first ones to ease you from all the howling and shouting,
They try their very best to make every precious life last,
With their efforts which are unsurpassed,
Hearing a newbie's first cry to an ailing one's last,
They appreciably manage the contrast,
Bringing sunshine to a new home,
They ensure smoothest delivery from a woman's womb,
Charming enough to stop a heartbeat,
And skilled enough to restart it again,
You call them doctors, I call them "miracle workers of life".

OUR LUNGS

Our body is a machine with so many amazing parts,
Yet we find the streets crowded with so many broken hearts,
The lungs of our body are no exception,
As is true that any obscurity can destroy their sheer perfection,
Having those little alveoli who run around exchanging the used-up carbon dioxide with fresh clear oxygen;
Which is no less than a work of an artisan,
Like a high tech pump our diaphragm pulls air into balloon like lungs,
Making the alveoli go to work;
Just like the latter being the former's clerk,
So many people insert harmful smoke into their lungs on purpose;
Unaware of the fact that its function is multi-purpose,
We're gifted with this incredible, wonderful and oxygen filled life;
Which undoubtedly is a rare rife.

FORCE MAJEURE (ACT OF GOD)

It seemed as if the Almighty was in no mood to be mighty,
I had to remind myself that I was the perfect Aphrodite,
As the pandemic worsened,
We all felt getting somewhat burdened,
Sufferings, fatalities, volcanic eruptions, destruction everywhere,
Huge queues of people to buy cylinders filled with the air,
It was an unmerciful disaster,
Which could be won only at the will of the Master.

THE STORM

Finding her ship stuck amidst a storm,
She didn't know what went wrong,
Craving for the guidance of her Captain,
It all seemed to her as comprehending Latin,
Failing to fathom the initial results,
Hitherto; everyone envisaged her to conduct herself as an adult,
She seemed hopelessly optimistic,
For the situation seemed highly sadistic,
They said every night is followed by a sunlight,
For it was only the Lord that could provide her with some respite,
Finally! The sea was calm and there was no storm,
Because her Captain was back to guide her in form.

APRIL DAY

Easy, carefree and a simple day,
Until she realized all wasn't okay,
Ninety five, ninety, eighty five to eighty,
Every breath of her Father was getting weighty,
For her Mother's eyes glued with pain just like any other wife,
Longing only for her husband's long life,
It was such an unfavorable situation,
For she had to bear all the exasperation,
Looking up to God to illuminate our way;
Without any delay,
For it was the force of his blessings that helped them through that miserable "April Day".

WAVE OF EMOTIONS

What is this wave of emotions?
Hurt! Sadness! Grief! Joy! Pain!
That eternally refuses to leave,
Whose adeptness the heart and the brain equally deceive,
It is very easy to avoid them the moment they happen,
For it was my belief that was misshapen,
A girl who was once a winner; seemed all lost,
Like a tree in late December withered and exhaust,
She yearned for a hand on her shoulder to help her get through the day,
She knew it that the God would soon illuminate her way,
Dismissing all the commotion,
She prayed with full devotion,
She believed that any moment a magic could happen,
For her personality was bold enough and resilient,
And soon she shone brilliant.

SOMEDAYS

Somedays I smile,

Somedays I cry,

Somedays are hard as rock,

Somedays are soft as clay,

Somedays life is kind,

Somedays life is pined,

Somedays are terrible,

While others are unbearable,

Somedays things will work out,

Somedays they won't,

For we must never disregard,

No matter how exceptionally the day is hard,

Somedays will make you wonder if amidst all the gloom,

If there is hope?

But you have to get up and find the rope,

Somedays you will end up crying for hours and hours,

That's when your only rescue will be belief in superpowers and miracle showers,

Take everything as the Almighty's sign,

Because every night is followed by a sunshine,

No matter how melancholous be the reason,

For each day is a new season.

BABY STEPS

What makes success at times delayed?
And then we are nothing; but all scared and afraid,
The secret is hidden in small baby steps consistently taken day by day,
And it is sure to repay in a merry way,
Don't visualize the series of steps and apprehend your climb,
Your baby steps would someday surely ring the success's wind chime.

COMFORT AMIDST CHAOS

Tired of all the hustles,

I rested at the Lord's feet all my troubles,

They thought it wasn't a big deal,

For I wanted to know;

How would the ailment heal?

I knew it; that it wasn't that simple,

Hitherto, the Lord granted me a symbol.

Comfort amidst chaos

When she come across a Genie,

My worries turned teeny,

The eyes which used to be filled with fears,

Overflowed with tears,

For it displayed gratitude;

For all her remaining years.

PARENTS

As kids we assume our parents to be blessed with super powers,
For it is them who make all the flowers fall on us as golden showers,
Just like you and me they too are mortal beings,
Their every decision has some or the other meaning; surrounded by a wise teaching,
They whole heartedly forgive all your sins,
Because they crave only to see you win,
They know the harshness of the world outside,
That is why they say, "Child beware of being caught by the high tides",
Their decisions may be right or wrong,
But their intention is always to make us strong,
For if they had the power to write your destiny,
It would have been like the one written by a Genie!

INSECURITY

The slightest thought of your place getting filled up with a void,
Within fractions of second it got me completely destroyed,
Crippling inside with insecurity; every moment felt like running a half marathon,
For I had to bear the burden of any error; whereupon,
Just like a termite slowly eating a piece of wood,
I longed for a heart that actually understood,
Unaware of being silently shielded with God's bulletproof jacket,
No amount of comforting phrases could get me out of that bracket,
I sank deeper and deeper in that pool of insecurity,
Externally depicting all the possible aspects of maturity.

ROUGH SPANS

For a moment everything seemed as if it came to a stand,
There came the foreplay of destiny,
Which said, 'Nothing is promised but definitely planned',
For a moment I felt the war within me would soon enter its coffin,
But it was a rough span which the Lord had decided to harden
before it could soften.

SLEEPLESS NIGHTS

Blindly staring at the walls of the room,
Which had lost all the bloom,
Sitting still by the fence of the wall,
Unguarded by a shawl,
Her vigilant eyes told a story,
Which lacked in its glory,
Adjusting her posture to save her back from an ache,
It was the darkness of the night that portrayed the intensity of her heartache,
Days, weeks, months elapsed,
But she still wasn't relaxed,
Within a blink of an eye,
Who knew from April it was July,
Reminiscing all the nights that now are a story of the past,
Hitherto, she got the sleep that was unsurpassed.

EXCRUCIATING PAIN

Seeing all her efforts going in vain,

She could no more bear that excruciating pain,

Swimming in a pool full of sharks,

Her soul was releasing silent sparks,

She did not know where to go,

For every moment was giving her a new blow,

Finding herself sandwiched between both her life lines,

Every tick of the clock was hitting her like fault lines,

She yearned for her Mother's lap,

But she had to respect the two - feet gap.

JUST ONE MORE TIME

Gazing at the twinkling stars,
Under the night sky,
Dejected eyes almost losing it to a loud cry,
Suddenly a little voice whispered, 'Just one more time', let's give it a try,
For the Lord surely won't deny,
Be stubborn enough to win,
When you've not committed any sin,
The Lord is sure to test you from within,
Be fierce enough to face the thick and the thin,
The fear is just to stay your try,
For you must be zealous for another try.

SINE QUA NON (WITHOUT WHICH NOTHING)

Being the sine qua non of our world,
Without you it's all dim and blurred,
The moment the machine used to stop its hum,
It used to turn me all numb,
The night of your absence O' Father was no less than an incision,
For I remember each hour of that night with great precision,
Unable to stop myself from drowning in the sea of grief,
For my every breath echoed that, "You're my only relief"!

SHOOTING STAR

Imagining of a lovely, unique and beautiful shooting star,
My heart and brain were constantly at war,
Standing under the sky full of stars,
I dreamt of a shooting star,
For it could only possibly remedy my invisible scar,
Within a blink of an eye,
There came a shooting star up in the sky,
With folded hands and closed eyes,
I prayed for a miracle,
Biblical, clinical and medicinal,
Silently fearing if it went unanswered,
For shooting stars are astronomical instances of a prayer being answered.

SITUATIONS

Amidst various walks of life,
Many a times we find ourselves stuck in situations we wish never existed,
We wish we had the force to get them blacklisted,
When they appear to as unacceptable,
They end up making us susceptible,
God or bad, happy or sad, every situation is masked with a hidden meaning,
Which in future requires a thorough screening,
Dealing with the complexities of life every day,
We end up in situations where we realize how stuck we have become in every way,
Craving every moment for all sorts of glory,
But isn't it only the one side of the story?
For our heart knows the truth behind the cock and the bull story,
Pump in a few deep breaths,
As these situations are only an interplay between life and death.

STATUS QUO (THE EXISTING STATE OF AFFAIRS)

Hours, minutes, seconds, weeks, days elapsed,
But they weren't relaxed,
It seemed like an uncontested race,
Which lacked its grace,
Worned out with the unusual routine,
Situation had become highly unforeseen,
For the day count had already reached fifteen,
Wondering at the Lord's will of maintaining status quo,
They didn't know where to go,
For it was the Lord's test of patience preparing them for a later glow.

QUESTIONS > ANSWERS

Questions have a certain way of testing your patience,

For it's your call to respond with abeyance or impatience,

Her eyes had become a wet desert,

Which had forgotten how to revert,

Seeking the answers to her never ending questions,

With pure intentions,

She reminded herself a lock isn't made without a key,

She mustn't flee,

Instead just be,

The Universe is sure to serve when the time is right,

No matter how dark the night,

For someday things are sure to be bright,

Because in the end everything eventually becomes alright.

TSUNAMI OF SALTY RIVERS

Eyes that always had a shine of a diamond,
Depicted a tsunami of salty rivers full of ions,
From sunset to sunrise,
Every moment she had to be prepared for a bitter- sweet surprise,
Unable to buy the desired relief,
She saved herself every time from drowning in the sea of grief,
For the world told her to keep up her faith and believe,
Night when her Captain was not here,
Pain was such excruciating; unable to bear,
Trying to overcome the darkness of the night with a sleep,
But all she could do was weep, weep and weep,
Her soul was getting silent shivers,
For the eyes had brought in a tsunami of salty rivers.

OH MY GOD!

The most used three letter word,
Oh my God!
Different situations give it a different impression,
Sometimes it is the mode to express our exhilaration,
Sometimes it is the only word when in aggression,
God is our first call; no matter what the situation,
For there is no particular definition,
Seeing her Captain's breath sinking,
She uttered Oh my God! without thinking,
Making a silent prayer for his suffering's deletion,
God soon decided to change her season,
Overjoyed to see him walking and talking,
She exclaimed Oh my God! you're rocking.

UNRESTRAINED STRENGTH

That look in his eyes,

That urge to fight all the impossibly possible fights to find a life,

The days kept passing on and on,

Two, four, six, eight, ten,

I did not know how and when,

The days and nights both seemed equally longer,

But his unrestrained strength grew stronger and stronger,

My questions and callouts were left unanswered,

But his unrestrained strength each time whispered,

'Child, don't you assume your Captain as weak'; no matter how absurd.

WHAT'S ENOUGH?

Etymologically implying an extent that is necessary,
But is it discretionary?
Constantly enthralled in the urge to keep on going,
It seems to be a fuzzy supposition of endlessly exerting,
What is enough?
Once it gets too rough and heavy,
What degree of patience do I endure?
Without uttering phrases that sound obscure,
To learn there isn't a cure,
What amount of hope shall I possess?
To not end up depressed,
What extent is goodness am I supposed to show?
To not experience a bad blow.

GRAVITY

All of us carry a disguised burden of damage,
Which we eternally fail to manage,
It's not the burden that we're afraid to feel,
But what we ultimately fail to conceal,
Maybe that is why sunny moments don't dive in that deep,
For there are tearful moments to make a clean sweep.

BELIEVE IN YOURSELF

Be yourself for the world is already taken,
For you're human; also be assured of being mistaken,
All that matters is your faith must be unshaken,
The road before her was a ribbon stretching across the desert,
But she never compromised on her effort,
Evidently ignoring her health,
Her every step was aimed at safeguarding her parent’s breath,
With consistent efforts they did the impossible,
For faith in God makes everything possible,
She salutes her Captain's unbridled strength,
It was his grit that made her safeguard his breath.

RANDOM ACTS OF KINDNESS

Kindness - as many may call it a little good luck charm,
That keeps you protected from all the harm,
Once it gets deeply embedded in your heart,
No matter what; it cannot depart,
A simple act of kindness is enough to make all the difference,
Soon you'll find the Universe arranging them in a sweet new sequence,
Always believe in acts of kindness; by way of spreading smiles,
For you never know it could travel a thousand miles,
I wonder if it holds a hidden message behind?
By virtue of those random acts of kindness it automatically gets defined,
Intertwined with gentleness and love,
It is the only means by which you can rise above.

PURE INTENTIONS

Pure intentions always count,

Because there is God to keep the account,

Sideline the ones who do not pay attention,

And religiously follow the path of pure intentions,

They say a tooth for a tooth,

But you don't have to evidence your truth.

DESTINY

Curious to learn what the future has for you in store,
You choose various methods to explore,
Contacting an astrologer to monitoring planetary variations,
You fear even minor deviations,
We depend on the planets of the solar system,
To learn if our health and finances would be in a good position,
Their movements hint us of our answers regarding marriage and commitment,
But it requires us to be patient,
For it comes with various flavours of entanglement,
The future by its virtue remains undeclared,
For it is not to make us scared,
But rather prepared,
Watch how the destiny's pen etches on the skin of your heart,
Because it is its one of the best works of art.

WANTS

In times of pain you ask for nothing but to be seen,
You are even labelled as being mean,
You want your existence to be felt,
But there's no way you can make the other melt,
You end up craving for them just when they leave,
There's no doorway even to a temporary relief,
You want them to feel your essence,
For it takes absence to value presence.

SATURATION POINT

When your soul's tolerance has reached the highest peak,
Somewhere you're sure to fall weak,
When everything appears dim and blurred,
Sit tight and wait until some hope finally gets transferred,
Maybe the cosmos is taking all the time,
To get the trappings aligned before it gets all fine,
Believe in the beauty of miracles,
For it could be wrapped up as chemical (medicinal) or physical (in the form of being).

MATURITY

What is this maturity?
Does it mean hurting less or is it being too strong?
Who decides whether you are right or wrong?
Age doesn't define your maturity that is for sure,
It requires your motives to be clean and pure,
You behave differently with every one,
To you it looks like a fun,
And you are a completely different person when it comes to that beloved one!
For there exists only one white balloon and one golden Sun,
Does crying make you immature?
Owing to the fact that somethings have no cure; it's better to endure,
Your maturity will make you deal with every situation in a different manner,
But never embrace the dark for its glamour,
The moment you cry for someone,
Behave like a kid,
Silently fight your battles,
Without anyone knowing even a bit,
You're labelled as mature,
No matter how obscure,
There is a little child in each one of us,

That fears coming out because the world knows how to make it a fuss,
Only the very special ones get to witness that child,
Who sometime smiles and sometimes gets too wild,
Caring for others, living for others, finding happiness in all the colors is maturity,
As these are the different symbols of depicting purity,
Feel happy when you see someone smile,
For being the reason behind someone's smile never goes out of style.

ANGER

Let your anger speak,
But you must learn how to use your beak,
Because it is sure to depict that you are weak,
Phases where you feel are all caught up by misery and depression,
Being angry is your only way of expression,
The world expects you to show your best trait,
But you just can't resist that boiling hate,
You want to run away from the flashbacks of all sorts of terrible thoughts,
But it is not possible unless you have fought,
If you continue to maintain that frown,
You're sure to drown,
Have your favorite cup of ice -cream,
You'll soon see your anger going,
Weak and turning into a broken beam,
Once you reach that healing wheel,
You'll find it isn't very hard to deal,
Just as every question paper has an answer key,
Every problem also has a solution,
You just made the innocent ones pay for your deconvolution.

MISTAKES

Mistakes - there aren't any such takes,
For there are only takes and retakes,
Mistakes are a proof that you are trying,
Instead of doing all the crying,
Mistakes are often punished with the tight slap,
For you understand the reason only after a reasonable time gap,
Gobbles you up throughout your time of test,
Making you give in the end your very best,
They make you learn the life's toughest lessons,
Minimizing the chances of future transgressions.

FAILURE

Its failure that brings out the best,
For you do not have to worry about the rest,
Like an ant never giving up on herself,
You must have enough faith in yourself,
Do not be dejected if your life is lacking that rhyme,
Both the Sun and the Moon shine in their own time,
For you must keep your efforts aligned,
Don't curse the failure,
Let your force within be your only savior.

YOU ARE YOUR OWN MAGIC

When situations are tragic,
And you fail to comprehend the logic,
Try and be your own magic,
Accept the challenges and take it as the Universe's adventurous ride,
Believe that the Almighty is all by your side,
Let your unshakable faith in him be your only guide,
Teachings of your Guru should be the principles you must abide,
For the bitter sweet moments are the ones that make this life worth a fight.

RAINBOW OF HOPE

The world is built on hope,
That's the beauty of the rainbow of hope that irrespective of the weather it helps us cope,
Until you let yourself loose the rope,
Composed of seven different colors,
They seem as second - hand lovers,
The moment you feel it's getting as bleak as the night,
For a rainbow is followed by a ray of sunlight,
Be courageous enough to find your rainbow,
That's the only way you'll ever find your lost glow.

SILENT PRAYER

A prayer is the most beautiful verse that makes your day truly refined,
The essence of miracles lie in the notes defined,
A silent prayer from a sincere heart is all you need to be lifted,
For it is the most valuable armoury that the Lord has gifted,
Longing to be rescued from the malignancy and the world's other fierce demons,
All you need is a silent prayer and persistent faith that never weakens.

THE PROBABILITY OF POSSIBILITY

Life is a spectrum of infinite possibilities,
For we are too focused only on the probabilities,
Once you decide to trust the possibility of something,
The Universe would never let you lose it to nothing,
Just as there is a rainbow only after rain,
You gotta believe in the existence of Ibiza when you are in Spain,
She surrendered her hope to impossibility,
That's when the Lord signaled her of a possibility,
Possibility always supersedes probabilities,
Which is how the Universe paves way for the facilities, activities and divinities.

THE FIRST MEET

Meeting you was no less than a miracle,
I knew it that it was clinical,
My concerns and worries resembled a spiracle,
And all that my lips wanted to express was way too lyrical,
Your eyes frowned in anger,
I wondered who is this weird stranger?
It was our first meet,
Which did not go any sweet,
Because you were overloaded with excessive heat,
I might fall short of words to describe,
But 'The first meet' will always have its own pride.

DECISIVE NIGHT

Confused between various this and that's,
Gazing bluntly at all the available stats,
I kept thinking whether to listen to my head or heart,
What if my decision broke everything apart?
I wanted to erase all my troubles,
For I was too tired of all the struggles,
Repeatedly getting swayed by external voices,
I knew it for a fact, I did not have many choices,
For it was that one decisive night,
That turned out the reason of everything soon being bright and alright.

VENOM EXCHANGED TO DRUG

Gazing at the earth through the rain,
I was struggling to overcome the unguarded pain,
I looked up to God for guidance, strength and security,
Soon I was rewarded with chants and jungles,
It was your footsteps that turned "venomous virus to a drug of surety".

SECRET DREAM

Astonished at the uncertainties of life,

He did not know until when will he be alive,

For he had fought the worst demon to survive,

Witnessing his girl who was brought up like a princess,

Not losing her strength amidst the biggest mess,

He crowned her of having achieved that secret dream,

For the situation was too extreme.

MY SHIVA

The laws of the God work in mysterious ways,
No matter how hard the days,
Don't worry about your circumstances,
Take them as his chances,
For you to discover your inner strength,
Which has been hidden in depth,
He knows all your pain,
For your efforts did not go in vain,
Being the only witness of your sorrows,
He has already scripted your happy tomorrow.

MY GURU

When the clouds of sadness hovered over her,

When nobody was there; you were,

She never believed in the intensity of your blessings,

Hitherto; she discovered that they had eliminated all her sufferings,

Slowly drowning in the pool of self-strife,

Your spirituality rescued her from life's toughest ride,

Forever looking up to you as my guide,

'My Guru', I am indebted to you for my whole life.

THIS TOO SHALL PASS

Brain filled with all sorts of doubt,
I wanted to shout out loud,
Silently dying inside in pain,
All her efforts were going in vain,
Everyone made their own forecasts,
Where there were many contrasts,
She knew that the phase was temporary,
As the issue was contemporary,
Whenever she found herself triggered,
'This too shall pass' was the slogan her heart whispered.

BE A WARRIOR NOT A WORRIER

When you find yourself trapped amidst a vicious cycle,
Which deals with question of your survival,
Be a warrior not a worrier.
Let your Mother's prayers be your hoodie,
The outcome is sure to be all goodie,
Let your Father's teachings be your dagger,
You 're sure to come out a swagger,
Disease, suffering, virus, opponent;
Irrespective of what or who needs
to be defeated,
No matter how you're treated,
Never mistake getting too heated,
Believe in the intensity of your fate,
For its surely going to surprise you mate,
Strike out the word fear from your dictionary,
Because your fate is far more than ordinary.

DOUBLE ROLE

Princess of her house,

Eyes glued at saving her Mother's spouse,

The mornings were not that bright,

For she had to be prepared for each and every fight,

May be that was the only way,

Things could ever be made alright,

She forgot herself with each passing day,

Silently craving for a voice to question if she was okay,

It was fear that drove her to action,

For God was ready to surprise her each time with a different reaction,

The world assumed that she was at peace,

Little did they know; she begged every second for her troubles to cease,

The nights were no less than a prison,

For the midnight curfew made her wait for the time until the Sun's arisen,

The night sky was as black as coal,

For the only thing that flew through her veins was if her Father's breath is in control,

Sitting unblanketed with folded feet,

For without him they felt totally incomplete,

Laying by the wall's fence,

The pain was getting deep and intense,
Like a voiceless infant craving for a Mother's lap and lullaby,
For that seemed the only way her sufferings could nullify,
Only to save those two hearts that God knitted into a single precious soul,
With relentless morning and night shifts she justified every role.

How > Why

What is the most natural reaction when something good or bad happens?
We say, 'Why me'?
For we never say, 'What is it trying to teach me'?
Sometimes the way things happen,
Is what we couldn't imagine,
It's the 'how' that becomes so strong,
Not letting you to recognize your own wrong,
7 BILLION PEOPLE
7 BILLION DIFFERENT CHOICE OF WAYS
Says a great deal about their intentions,
For it's too terrible to mention,
By and large the toughest calls of life,
Mostly which are strife,
Could be taken in more gentler ways,
For it could ease out someone's harsh phase.

BE A GIVER

He always taught her to be a giver in life,
No matter how hard it made you strive,
Have a heart that never hardens,
Do not shy away from seeking your pardons,
Always do a good deed with a clean heart,
The Almighty silently drops a blessing in your cart,
Nothing better than this makes him happy,
For if the Almighty's happy you would never be unhappy.

SILENCE IS VOCAL

How often do we freely seek to speak?
Only a handful of times; only to preserve the silence from any leak,
Yet many a times our tongues are tied,
Your words elude and hide,
Keeping the wave of emotions within,
Little talks amidst the head and the soul begin,
Merely a shadow of hope persists,
To help us overcome the Universe's upcoming twists,
You think those quiet; have nothing to say?
What if it's only a fake display?
Ever wondered what did the sweet silence last say?

OOPS > WHAT IF'S

In a world full of what if's,
Ever tried being an oops?
Moments you have been eagerly waiting for are finally here,
Carpet it with an oops if you feel even a tiny bit of fear,
You tried but you never cried,
Lest you know you would have been fried,
This fear of failure made you cry and hide,
For it was nothing more than a low tide,
Ever tried being an oops?
You ruined it, because instead of breaking the spin of loop; you drowned yourself in the soup.

DEEP WITHIN ME

The voice I hear within myself,
Is synonymous to the one echoing within you,
I wonder if it's really true?
Audible even from a great distance,
I am unable to deny its existence,
The voice I hear within myself,
Is synonymous to the one echoing within you,
It enlightens my path for tomorrow,
Restricts my thoughts from being narrow,
So what if it comes with a little sorrow?
In no case would it be higher than Mt Kilimanjaro!

COURAGE

No matter what life throws at you,
Always have the courage to face the view,
For that is followed by a very few,
Irrespective of whether you are in tandem or alone,
Have the courage to overcome the monotone,
Never hesitate to fight for your vanity and pride,
Have the courage to dismiss all negations and digress all melancholy,
For that's the norm you must always abide.

DELAYED JUSTICE

Frustrated and deceived at the play of the fate,
Unable to resist further her sorry state,
Every moment her heart prayed only for peace,
But each time her anguish and exasperation increased,
She begged the Universe to enlighten her footsteps,
Soon which were followed by concrete steps,
For they soon worked like magic,
Which released her from all the possible panic,
It was only justice that was delayed,
That made her all afraid.

FEELING OF RELIEF

Waiting to experience that feeling of relief,
When the Lord would free her from that grief,
From seeing her parents breathe abnormally,
To finally seeing it change to normally,
The Lord blessed her with that 'Feeling of Relief',
Which later became the reason for strengthening in him her belief.

REBIRTH

Almost losing the count of your breath,
You were almost near to death,
Some say it is the drug that worked on you,
Others say it was a bad omen that escaped you,
Many others say it was only a miracle that saved you,
For irrespective of whatever came true,
I believe it was a "rebirth" that the Almighty gave you.

HEYDAY!

Finally!
It was the most awaited day,
For where there is a will; there is always a way,
Ears that yearned to hear your voice,
Could now rejoice,
Eyes that only saw you sleeping,
Could now see you speaking,
For it was undoubtedly the best feeling,
My heart craved to hear only one line,
That now, 'I am fine',
For soon you made me jump and reach cloud nine,
Who says it was an ordinary day?
Innumerable silent and pure prayers made it a 'Heyday' as many may say.

SUCCESS

How would you define success?
To a rich man it may be having a big car,
To an actor it may be becoming a superstar,
To a poor man it may be getting his family two square meals a day,
To a child it may be his Mother allowing him to play,
To every person the meaning is different,
We work all our lives to earn the desired name and fame,
For that ends up being our life's only aim,
But isn't that way too lame?
From morning shifts to night shifts we are too absorbed in building wealth,
At the expense of our valuable health,
More often than not it is said successful people "eat well",
But a little less successful people definitely "sleep well",
Find success is the little things of life,
For they're the ones you're forever going to rejoice,
Don't lose yourself in the race to win life's competitions,
Real success lies in helping one another irrespective of the situation,
You'll reap the fruits of the hard work, you deserve,
Never let your morals and principles take a swerve,
Elucidate the term according to whatever makes you think is right,
But never stop being humble and polite,
For success is surely going to be your next flight.

HAPPINESS

What is the doorway to happiness?
For it definitely is your very own choice,
Which you must rejoice,
Happiness is something that comes from within,
Do not expect it to be found if you have played with the sin,
Ever wondered how beautiful and young you look when smiling?
Stay away from things that infect and contaminate your happiness,
For it is only going to leave you with emptiness,
Everyone is busy pretending to be happy,
But is it that, that they are truly happy?
From a teenager struggling with a complicated relationship to an old man fighting an ailment,
From a debt ridden person trying to arrange finance,
To a rich businessman trying to attain work life balance,
Everyone is juggling with some or the other malaise,
Which is different from the other in various ways,
Learn to be the controller and master of your own happiness,
For you deserve all the joy, love and cheerfulness,
Let yourself have that indomitable faith,
That things would eventually fall into place,
Irrespective of the case,
Possess that skill of making everything amusing and interesting,
For you call it happiness, I call it, 'Medicine of the Soul'!.

BE YOURSELF

Having a head full of stories,
Trying to fly above all my worries,
When I looked down at my fears,
Which I had been hiding since many years,
I realized I had wasted countless tears,
Moments later I asked my heart,
Am I nearing my end or is it a new start?
For it whispered, that it being a small part; which shall soon depart,
Immersed in the winds of fate,
Unable to locate the exit gate,
I realized there exists the supreme power of God who alone is great,
So shed off all your limitations,
Be yourself, and live up to all your expectations.

FUTURE

Future is best left unpredicted,
That’s how the Universe keeps its plan encrypted,
Undoubtedly the plan of the Lord is well scripted,
It is not a parcel to be received,
It's rather a goal or height waiting to be achieved,
One might not see immediate results,
But that's no way our insult,
Owing to its unpredictability; it is customarily feared,
Instead of being reared,
It is not something to be taped,
But rather shaped and baked,
Is it a fair bargain or a promised deal?
None! A journey to be taken to know its feel,
It is not supposed to be annulled as oblique,
It's rather eager in anticipation for us to seek.

THE LAST SONG

I wanted to sing to you a song,
That come what may; the love is for sure to last long,
Your heart was the place I actually belonged,
For it was me; that you suddenly went all strong,
I wanted the song to play until I close my eyes in your embrace,
For you wanted to see the Sun's morning rays fall on my face,
I wanted to make the best of that song,
I knew it; that it was the last song.

LAST BREATH

What if I assumed my next breath to be my last breath?
For I cannot overcome the irrefutable fact of death,
It is synonymous to a fierce coercive threat,
What if I assumed for a nanosecond that my heart would soon be beating it's one last beat?
I'd allow my body and soul to soon release all its heat,
Because every last breath somewhere is a beginning to another anywhere,
So why do I need to fear that last breath?
Maybe because to many it would be more than cruelty; but to me 'death'.

LESSONS

When the lessons of life become harsh to the core,
Do not ignore and instead give it a roar,
You might feel broken amidst that fight,
For every dark night is followed by a ray of sunlight,
It's true that every lesson comes with a cost,
And there are a couple of things that too get lost,
Wisdom may a times gets replaced by mistakes,
Only the warriors know what it takes,
Lessons marked as soul fillers,
For they are the ones that end up making us the winners.

IMMENSE GRATITUDE

No matter what life throws at you,

Have an attitude of immense gratitude,

Hold on to this attitude even amidst life's toughest challenges,

For it is only to help us with all the checks and balances,

Your ingrate spirits and thankless attitude,

Will only extend your latitude,

So always have immense gratitude,

And the cosmos is sure to shower you with things much larger in their magnitude.

SELF-RESPECT

While walking on life's track,
Never part away with the possession of self-respect that has been placed on the rack,
Finding it hard to walk alone,
Her fragile heart longed for love from the known and the unknown,
Tired of hearing tantalizing words,
She decided to be her own herb,
Choosing the path that was right for her self-respect,
She believed in the possibility of things soon being alright without any further disrespect,
Patting her own back for being strong,
For she hadn't done any wrong,
The Lord bestowed her with all the bravery and power,
As he had then planned for her a grand happiness shower.

YOU ARE NO LESS THAN A STAR

Exploring each and every self-avatar,
Irrespective of whether a son or a daughter always believe that you are no less than a star,
Lest you wouldn't have come this far,
No matter if you are together or standing alone,
Have the conviction to face even the unknown,
For you're a star born to shine bright,
Irrespective of the day and the night.

CAUSE & EFFECT

"As the call so the echo",
So, who's in the saddle to maintain the count?
Beware! it's the Universe and the Almighty that are flawless at keeping the accounts,
What you do today,
Will determine whether your life will be pink or grey,
We're all caught up in the wheel of right and wrong,
Which will ultimately decide; where do we belong?
Never ending loop of good and bad, cause & effects,
May leave us only with regrets,
I believe karma isn't just done by body but also by thoughts,
For which you have to pay the costs,
It could be dressed as a curse or a blessing,
It stretches your lips into smiles if it's a blessing,
For its undeniably too refreshing,
It makes your chin down if it's a curse,
For now it's your time to reimburse;
"I didn't do it"! is your plea to the Universe,
But your heart knows the hidden truth behind the verse,
It's too easy to complain,
And be all in for a blame game,
Only to find yourself ending up with shame,
So, sit and analyze what was it that you did wrong,

Instead of singing your own sad song,
The Universe shall make you pay for your actions sooner or later,
Whose effect would be much -much greater,
Every morning is a new day,
Which is in your hands to make it grey or a heyday,
Forgive yourself for being wrong,
Remember it for making you strong,
Let yourself be guided by the force to make your journey an inspiration,
Let it be the mode of your identification,
For you never know who would make you the reason behind their motivation,
Anyone dealing with the similar state of affairs,
Shall know the gateway to the stairs and all the possible repairs,
Have faith as strong as the power of a blank cheque,
For there is the "Law of Karma" to keep you in check.

REALIZATIONS

Drenched in the pool of uncertainty,
Look up to God to heal you with serenity,
Soon everything that is important will be crystal clear,
Which will release you from all the possible fear.

A BAD DREAM

Last night she had a dream,

As bad as it could seem,

Little did she know,

Day by day she was losing all her glow,

Today when she looks back a chill runs down her spine,

She closely squeezes her Mother until she gets fine,

For it may be insane to believe,

That illness and griefs in nightmares only deceive.

SILENT TREMORS

Stroke me gently,
Listen to me intently,
There's still a monster from my past,
Which makes me aghast,
Resting in the little corner of my dead drag heart,
Each time it returns; it tears me apart,
The visuals run within my veins as fault lines,
The memories that keep applying reverse gears hit me like an aftershock after an earthquake,
What is the cause of this destruction?
For my soul is still under construction.

THE HEART AND THE SOUL

Admiring the beauty of the world,
Which in myriad ways remains to be unfurled,
It seemed to me,
That there are bazillion of ways to just be,
For I was supposed to remember,
That my heart cannot be a naked tree as in late December,
I can be all rattling and invincible,
Because even the cosmos tries to make the most ambitious and admirable as unsinkable,
Seven billion people, seven billion different ways,
Umpteen opinions yet confine days,
Every page shall reveal some story,
Irrespective of my failures and setbacks it shall be my glory,

Regardless of what in life you choose,

Put your heart and soul in whatever you do irrespective of whether you 'win or lose'.

SKEPTICISM

An impulse so frequent that I always ignore,
Maybe it's something I am not gonna hold back anymore,
For it was like rising and falling tides getting scored,
Why am I too skeptical about my every move?
What is it that my heart every time disapproves?
I consider my miseries as big and intense,
But I was the only one at my defense,
For maybe my helplessness made no sense,
The waves of confusion were always ready to sweep me away,
But all I needed was some time to make a way.

TRUST

A trust once broken can never get things back to normal,
All it does is to end things with echoing words of quarrel,
Don't forget to be loyal to the ones around,
Lest you'll be drowned,
Fed up of listening to lies,
I sunk in the pool of incessant cries,
The world is selfish,
You need to make your own ways,
Irrespective of the number of days,
Be strong enough to handle things on your own,
Lest amidst a calamity you will be a complete unknown,
Never make promises when you are happy,
Because your inability to keep them ahead is sure to make you unhappy,
In life when you make any relation,
Maintain enough trust and communication without any expectation,
If you hold any hand,
Make sure you make even the toughest storm withstand,
Never try and break anyone's trust,
For God is sure to dismiss you with disgust.

HOME IS WHERE HEART IS

Home is where heart has no fear,
Home is where heart is tender and clear,
Different people may define home to them differently,
For it may be based on their experience inherently,
For me home is where my Mother can cook me a meal,
It is enough for me to get the desired zeal,
For me home is where my Father comes back after the day's hustle,
It is enough for my heart to know he's there to keep me away from all the struggle,
For me home is where I can play all my favorite songs,
It is enough to know I am not doing any wrong,
For me home is where I can silently prepare for my future goals,
It is enough for my heart to get the glimpse of my future roles,
For me home is where I can gossip with my friends for hours and hours,
It is enough to free my heart of all the possible scars.

EVERYTHING OR NOTHING?

More often than not; you suppose you know everything in order to succeed,
Inevitably constraining and limiting yourself only to mislead,
Desist from letting your confidence in your competencies reduce to a mere dot,
For that's how you'll end up fetching a lot,
Your education and learning might get you win based on logic,
But what if accepting knowing nothing could make in some place for some magic?
Knowledge and mindfulness is supreme to make sense,
For the reality is sometimes too mystical and dense,
Just as everything emerges from nothing and vice versa,
Do we really know everything?
Or maybe knowing nothing is sometimes the only way to know everything.

EXTERNAL VALIDATIONS

We live our lives searching and craving for words of affirmation,
Lest we feel we're in negation,
Which ends up being the reason of our frustration,
Absence of these words also makes us feel insufficient,
Does it also make us less efficient?
Willingly putting our worth in the hands of others,
Unaware of the fact that they're all suckers,
We keep yearning for all sorts of external validations from them,
Which is soon followed by a harsh retaliation which they immediately condemn,
Unable to control the action of others,
We still continue to yearn,
In the long run it only ends up making us stern,
Preferring the opinions of others over your own,
Will only make your urge for external validations more grown,
Its sure to take you down a very difficult path,
Because you'll become your own wine of wrath.

RUMORS

Rumors are rumor for a reason,
They spread irrespective of the season,
The one spreading knows all the truth,
Unaware of the fact that it could mar his youth,
Irresistible is the fact that you are flawless and they can never degrade you,
Either ways rumors are trusted by a very few,
Smile! If you see a rumor around,
For your life is what their brain always surrounds,
Your loved ones know what the truth is,
And that its full of fizz,
Let them talk behind your back,
They are sure to be soon back on track,
Just know one thing for sure,
That if your intentions are pure,
No rumor would ever make you insecure.

TRUTH > LIES

Do not believe in what others say,
Find your own way,
Do not blindly believe what you see
For it might be the wrong key,
They might give up on you when you reveal your real side,
For your morals and principles should be your only guide,
When they realize you know the truth,
They start maligning the sooth,
You would be blamed for their sin,
But they know they are hiding a truth within,
The Universe knows that their actions weren't right,
Which will soon make them grieve at their own plight,
It's the real lies that break real ties,
For futile are all the future cries,
They want to keep their life all sorted,
For the 'Law of Karma' shall soon get them thwarted,
A bigger lie is always smaller when in the face of a smaller truth,
For that's the universal sooth.

FOREVER IS A LIE

What makes you think you won't get out of the miseries you're facing right now?
What makes you think it's a permanent damage to your life?
Nothing is permanent,
No one is permanent,
Forever is a lie,
Nothing stays forever,
You never know which could be your last moment with your loved ones however,
You feel impossible to get out of a struggle, But you must never give up your hustle,
You might think your heart would never heal,
For you must dismiss it being only a temporary feel,
Everything has an expiration date,
You must be ready to wait,
Do not confuse a phase for a lifetime,
Things unfold in their own way only at the right time,
Focus on your growth, life will change,
Initially it might sound strange,
For its well within your range,
Things eventually workout and you get stronger,
Though it might take a little longer,
There are times when being strong will be the only option you'll

have,

Irrespective of the circumstances do not calve,

Open your blindfolds and start living,

Because forever is a lie,

Life is all about forgetting and giving.

LOVE IS SACRED

What is love?
Assuming different forms in different roles,
It is something that never fails to touch a soul,
Different in different situations,
Devoid of a clear definition,
Often regarded as one of the greatest emotions,
I wonder; if it's only a drop in the ocean?
People who are connected heart to heart,
Can never be made apart,
God is the reason behind those relations,
For where love is sacred; it is sure to defeat all complications.

LINGERING

What is that, that you keep on lingering?
Why is it that each time you have to wait for the alarm bell to ring?
For this lingering will not help you learn anything,
You might fool yourself with a stomach ache,
In order to be on a leisurely break,
Your heart knows that it's all fake,
Lingering things because you are too afraid,
It's nothing but a fear self-made,
For which would surely get your success delayed.

MINI CHUNKS OF GUILT

Unable to blur that terrible cyst or sore in my brain,

It kept coming again and again,

It found pleasure in doing everyday rounds,

Unaware of the fact that I couldn't anymore afford those nervous breakdowns.

OPPORTUNITIES TOO RIOT

It is often said that opportunities seldom bang,
For it's our job to make them a part of our gang,
Ambivalent enough to take the either view,
Which may or may not be true,
They give us a warm cuddle,
Before they burst your illusionary bubble and gear you up for your upcoming struggle,
Silently dancing on the streets of your mind,
They ensure that the stars are well aligned,
Stirring up your dreams to save you from a possible grudge,
Notwithstanding the times you refuse to budge,
Hinting you to recall episodes of valor and courage once portrayed by a hidden girl,
Who is pure like pearl,
I believe opportunities don't bang; they either cordially or harshly stir you,
Ever realized of those petite instinctive sensations in your body,
Yeah! That's the tacit riot opportunities embody.

TOOTHLESS SWORD

Words, little words adept enough in making giant false claims,
Silently taking all the accusations as well as the blames,
Irrefutable is the fact that their force is intense,
Crawling through our mind they slay us with suspense,
Ambivalent enough to team them as buddies or enemies,
I believe them to be drunken blasphemies with no remedies,
Often regarded as a toothless sword,
It is none other than the Lord who saves it for the record.

INDIFFERENT

Often glaring at the beauty of the white balloon,
I wonder why is that that we admire only the beauty of the Moon?
For the eclipses equally affect both the Sun and the Moon,
The Sun seldom hides behind the clouds,
Maybe because it doesn't like saying it out loud,
It pretends well to look ordinary,
Often forgetting its way beyond extraordinary,
It pretends well to look fine,
We fail to understand; it is its sign,
Perhaps, it's too consistent,
And we are too indifferent.

MISFITS

You might feel many a times like a misfit,
For you must immediately dismiss it,
You are way more than anyone's sidekick,
Because you aren't a misfit,
But a wonderful soul wrapped in a bulletproof outfit.

ONE DAY

One day everything will change,
It might make you feel violent and strange,
Those who speak,
Will all be silent,
Be it youth or the aged,
The blissful or the suffering,
All shall be gone,
One day everything will change,
Maybe someday the future generations get to read it in history,
But with a touch of mystery,
We must remember they existed,
For they never deserved to be blacklisted.

IGNORANCE IS A BLISS

As a kid I always thought life was simple,

Easy carefree and full of miracles,

I didn't know what was fear,

Until I stood alone and nobody was near,

I didn't know pain,

Until I broke and could not maintain,

It started small,

Soon making me take a call,

Now that I know life,

I realized I was ignorant to all heartaches and strife.

DODGE THE CONVICTION

Avoidance is dodging the inevitable for instant gratification,
The instant gratification may sooth the sensation,
But you'll eventually have to pay the compensation,
It could be weeks, months or years later,
But you'll eventually have to answer the Creator,
Irrespective of the obstructions you take,
You must be able to save yourself from all the aches,
Beware of the number of adverse forces you are harvesting,
It is only the conviction each time that you are carpeting,
The pond of stress and anxiety you are suppressing in time,
Let me tell you buddy you're committing to yourself a serious crime.

NEW YEAR RESOLUTION 2022

With the hope for new beginnings today,
Let's untangle all knots of regret without any delay,
Promise to honor your resilience,
Which you've gained from immense experience,
Celebrate every tiny bit of your achievement,
Do not mistake it, to be a mere reprievement,
Believe! That you are an energy far greater than any ailment,
You are an unstoppable force; not worth any bereavement.

SOMEWHERE IN BETWEEN

Somewhere between what I used to be,
And what I am yet to become,
Old ancient ways of thinking dissolved,
For the time had now evolved,
And the riddles had to be solved,
New perspectives were yet to be formed,
I wish if I was warned,
But I found myself in the middle of nowhere,
And to say the least nowhere is still somewhere,
Maybe there was a hidden divine purpose,
Despite the fact I was nervous,
There was something very whimsical about the in - between which later turned out to be magical.

AN EVENT THAT CHANGED ME

I am not the same person I was way back; anymore,
For that one "EVENT" changed me to its core,
Amidst every crises lies some or the other hidden good,
You just gotta hang in there until its finally understood,
You can't be the same person who entered the storm,
Because that's how the Universe wants you to transform,
Astonished by the nuances of the world,
Each time I was swirled,
From unmasking various masked faces,
It made me a victim of numerous rages,
The "EVENT" left a forever crack in my heart,
For that's how the Universe had conspired to make me smart.

THANK YOU A BUNCH!

I wish I could thank everyone not once, not twice but a zillion times,

Though I can never explain my gratitude in a few lines,

Thank you to God for being my navigator,

For directing my footsteps to every possible elevator,

Thank you to the doctors for putting their life at stake,

For saving innumerable families from a possible heartbreak,

Thank you to the officials at the Ministry of Health,

For making your calls at regular intervals to ensure our well-being a reason for my strength,

Thank you to the Police Officers bearing the scorching heat on road,

For making the passage of hospital wagon unopposed,

Thank you to the medical staff that served us at home,

For making us feel we're not alone,

Thank you to everyone else directly or indirectly part of this arduous journey and phase,

I shall always fall short of ways to convey the intensity and amplitude of my praise.

www.ingramcontent.com/pod-product-compliance
Lightning Source LLC
LaVergne TN
LVHW050315160826
845677LV00014B/3404

* 9 7 8 9 3 5 4 4 6 8 0 2 5 *